VOYAGE
TO THE BOTTOM
OF
THE BED

Written by Connie Amarel
Illustrated by Swapan Debnath

ISBN 978-1-61225-034-2

Published by Mirror Publishing
Milwaukee, WI 53214

Printed in the USA.

This book is dedicated to my "Voyage to the Bottom of the Bed" partner, my sister Sandie, with much appreciation for her excellent ideas, suggestions and support. It is also dedicated to my dear friend, Dr. Alan Weber, with many thanks for his helpful insight and recommendations. Lastly, it is dedicated to my wonderful family for their continued love and support.

My little sis wouldn't take her nap,
she laughed and played instead.

Mom couldn't make her fall asleep,
so I climbed in her bed.

I rubbed my eyes and yawned real big,
then very quickly said,

She clapped her hands, jumped up and down,
"Oh yes, let's go!" she said.

So we lifted up the covers
and were off, full speed ahead.

To our right we saw a sea lion
gnawing on some bread.
And two dolphins swimming side by side
most certainly were wed.

When a school of fish swam toward us
filling both of us with dread,
we imagined hungry creatures
hoping soon they would be fed.

We both gasped as a shark swam by,
a great big hammerhead.
But that didn't stop our voyage
to the bottom of the bed.

We passed by snapping turtles
who looked over, then they fled.
While a jellyfish went floating by
and brushed against my head.

A large mouth bass sailed slowly by,
my sister named it Fred.

A hermit crab that didn't move
I think was playing dead.

In the distance sat an octopus
with eyes of blazing red.

It was staring at electric eels,
its tentacles were spread.

At the corner where a dragon slept
we very softly tread.

But that didn't stop our voyage
to the bottom of the bed.

We saw a shipwreck down below
and remnants of a sled.

A jacket wedged between the rungs
was made of silken thread.

We were having such a great time,
"Let's go on!" my sister plead.

With excitement we forged onward,
Wondering where this new path led.

But our flashlights both got dimmer
as the batteries went dead.

It was getting difficult to see
with light not being shed.

Just then my sister loudly snored.
"She's sound asleep!" Mom said.

And that's what stopped our voyage
to the bottom of the bed.

CPSIA information can be obtained at www.ICGtesting.com
Printed in the USA
LVIW01n0702110216
474625LV00003B/8